The
AURÒNA

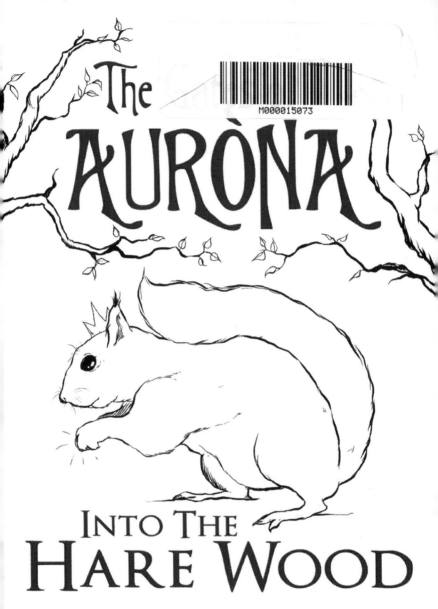

INTO THE
HARE WOOD

WRITTEN BY TONYA MACALINO

ILLUSTRATED BY MAYA LILOVA

CRYSTAL
MOSAIC
BOOKS

This is a work of fiction. All of the characters, organizations, and events portrayed in this novel are either products of the author's imagination or are used fictitiously.

INTO THE HARE WOOD
Excerpt: THE ANGUÀNA'S TALE

For information, address Crystal Mosaic Books, PO Box 1276 Hillsboro, OR 97123

ISBN: 978-0-9911061-9-6

Printed in the United States of America

For my own fearless adventurer,
Heléna.
My love, may you never lose
that bold curiosity...
or your love for small, furry animals!
–Tonya Macalino

With gratitude,
to *everyone,*
for their kindness.
–Maya Lilova

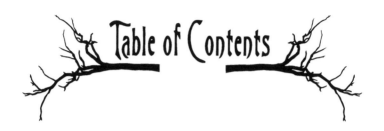

Table of Contents

List of Full Plates

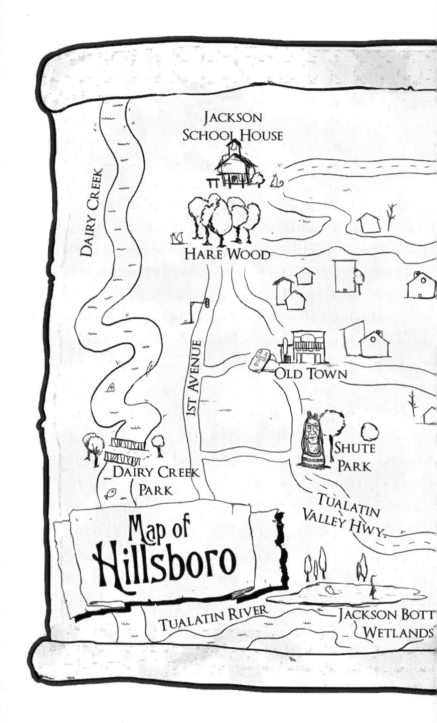

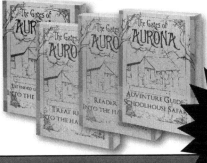

The Gates of
AURONA

INTO THE
HARE WOOD

For
Righley —

Be extraordinary!

LEAVES IN AN AUTUMN STORM.

Chapter One

An Autumn Storm in Summer

Pick up time at Jackson School Elementary always reminded Hannah Troyer of leaves in an autumn storm: colorful swirls streaming around each other, the roar of all of those leaf-bodies swishing past each other, straining to reach each other, getting swept away from each other.

And if you didn't watch out, one would smack you right in the face.

"Oh, my gosh! Hannah!"

Hannah blinked up from her new position flat on the sidewalk. Wonderful. The rocks from the concrete stung her palms as she carefully pulled her hands from the ground. Clark Talwar, her neighbor, reached down to help her up. Even wonderfuler. She tried to beat him to it, but her backpack had her tangled and she only ended up looking like a turtle flipped on its back with its legs swinging uselessly in the air. With a defeated sigh, she

let Clark pull her to her feet. Clark's big sister, Diana, brushed the rocks from her pack.

"Uh, thanks," she mumbled, turning quickly away.

Clark and Diana's mom, Apsara, hugged her giant gold purse to her chest like it was a wildcat threatening to attack again at any second. Her eyes were huge.

"Oh, Hannah, I am so sorry. Are you all right?"

Hannah rubbed her cheek and the side of her eye where Apsara had smacked her with the purse. That was when she spotted her mom, Bridget, just beyond the fake gold leather. Maybe she should have asked Apsara to hold her mom back, too.

Too late.

"Hannah-Bannah, holy fern frogs! Are you okay? Let me see your eye."

Hannah just used the offended eye to glare at her.

"It's fine."

Her mom started to pry her hand off the stinging mark. Hannah twisted away, joining a stream of leaf-bodies flowing toward the big oak. She'd just seen her big brother, Cameron, shoot past her in the middle of a wild game of Harry Potter tag. Cam and his

buddies could quote every spell in the series. They slammed into each other, shouting spells and counter-spells. Hannah kept well out of slamming range and waited for her mom to catch up.

In pairs and clusters, Hannah watched her classmates drift through the gates back to the playground.

One last after-school playdate.

One last goodbye to third grade. Next year would be the last year she and Cam would be in Jackson together; the last year they would be in any school together until she was a freshman in high school. *In high school!*

Hannah's tablemates, Rebekah and Asia, whispered and giggled as they disappeared around the corner toward the playground. *Liar, liar, pants on fire,* Hannah thought after the two biggest gossips in her class. She wrinkled her nose, but couldn't stop herself from gazing longingly at the corner where they'd disappeared.

Finally, her mom managed to pull herself away from the crowd of parents saying their goodbyes at the door.

"Mom, can we go to the playground?" Hannah asked.

Cam jogged up, breathless from his spell-casting.

"Yeah, Mom. Can we?"

Mom shook her cell phone at them.

"I got a job. We've gotta get home."

"But it's the last day of school! Please!" Cam pleaded. Hannah didn't bother. She knew those four words "I got a job" were a deal closer. And besides, not one of those backpacks bobbing past on the way to the gate had paused to invite her. Not like Cam's entire quidditch team which slouched in disappointment as he turned to follow their mother down the path toward home.

Hannah trailed along behind.

The sky glowed neon blue above them. Their mom steered them toward the shady path while most of the other kids, including Clark and Diana, went with Apsara and her giant gold purse down the main green space. Hannah sighed again and with a wave, turned away.

The first to greet them along the sidewalk was Snowy, a little lady of a cat, who welcomed

Hannah with a head-butt. This was a ritual even "I got a job" couldn't interrupt. The whole family, the whole neighborhood, knew Hannah was cat crazy. And dog crazy. And squirrel crazy. And bird crazy. And once she'd even found a baby mole.

It was safe to say she was animal crazy.

Except for snakes and spiders. She was not crazy about snakes and spiders.

Cam stopped to scratch Snowy on the chin. He was pretty much as cat crazy as Hannah was.

"It's going to be a lonely summer without Nicola," Cam said quietly.

"Yeah," Hannah agreed.

Their own cat had died just three weeks ago. It made their house kind of quiet, kind of empty without her sleek shadow following them everywhere.

"We'll visit you, Snowy, I promise," she whispered as the lady cat rubbed high against her leg.

Hannah gave Snowy one last scratch under the chin, soaking up all the love she could, and then ran to catch up to their mother.

Mom had stopped at the head of the street. She stared down the hill with a funny look on her face. Hannah and Cam grabbed the hands she offered and swung to a stop.

THEY'RE ALL HERE, HAN.

Cats.

More cats than she ever knew lived in the neighborhood—and she thought she knew them all.

At the bottom of each driveway for two blocks, maybe three, a cat sat at attention, ears trained forward toward the road. How weird. Hannah gripped her mom's hand a little tighter and her mom squeezed back.

"They're all here, Han. There's Furry. There's Peanut. There's Pickles. There's those two cats that chase each other across the roof every morning," Cam murmured.

Hannah nodded. "There's Pretty Kitty. There's Shadow. There's Peter Pan. And there's Mori! What's she doing so far from home?"

"It looks to me like you two have your own honor guard for the last day of school," Mom said, still not moving forward.

This was better than a playdate any day!

Hannah and Cam dragged their mother down to the first driveway. They gave Furry a good scratch behind his big black ears and picked a few dead leaves out of his thick coat. He began to purr, but he didn't move. Mom didn't let go of their hands.

They moved on to Peanut, an old gentleman cat with an orange-striped coat. Even after Hannah gave him his favorite chin rub, he didn't flop down and roll onto his back. He just stared forward and purred loudly.

Hannah looked up at her mom. Her mom looked down and shook her head.

"I have no idea."

The cats remained purring guardians like that all the way down to the main road. The school crowd had long disappeared by the time they got to the end. Together, they turned back to look up the road.

Their honor guard was gone.

"Um, where'd they go?" Hannah asked, her skin prickling strangely.

"Super weird," Cam agreed

Snowy stepped out from behind the corner hedge and gave them a loud "perrow." The prickling worry faded from Hannah's neck and arms. All three of them shifted and twisted as the white cat wound between their legs.

Snowy crossed the street and called to them with another loud "perrow" from the opposite corner.

"Okay, what are you up to, little girl?" Mom asked the cat. Now she was the one pulling Hannah and Cam forward. Hannah knew her Mom's reporter brain was on hyperdrive. Which was okay, because this time Hannah was pretty curious, too. What could make all the kitties in the neighborhood act like guards at the royal palace all at the same time? One of the things she loved about cats was their graceful play. This was so not right.

Mom released their hands on the other side of the road and they all jogged to catch up with the sleek, white cat as she trotted up the path. Hannah wished so desperately that she could dump her backpack. Filled with goodbye projects and presents, it slammed against her back with every step; soon, parts of her began going numb.

But Snowy didn't go far. She stopped just in front of the old school house—the office for the neighborhood association. Hannah had always thought the old building was cool with its school bell, the big porch covered with hanging flowers, and the hitching post out

NOW, IF ONLY THE HITCHING POST HAD HORSES.

front. Now, if only the hitching post had horses actually hitched to it...

"What? Need a cat to remind you to pay the dues?" Cam joked to their mother.

"Very funny. This is just too weird," Mom said as she dug into her tiny purse. "I actually do need to stop here..." She finally got hold of the phone and scrolled quickly through it. "...Yes, the Jackson School House. That's so weird."

Mom bent down and gave Snowy a thank you stroke down the back, wandering distractedly forward, starring at her phone.

Mom pushed the doorbell. In reply, the door buzzed and unlocked with a pop. Mom held the door for them as they went in. Hannah followed Cam past the antique bookcase and through a doorway framed in stained glass to a single room about twice the size of their living room. She'd only been in the school house a couple times before, but she'd always found the old wood comforting—like it held the memories of the kids from the old days with their big-skirted dresses and their trousers with the wide suspenders. And their bonnets and hats—those were cool.

"Imagine if all the kids in the neighborhood—all the way up through high school—fit in this one room. Over there in the corner would be the woodstove and up there would be the one teacher you all shared."

"All the way through high school?" Hannah asked. Now, that sounded scary—being in with the big kids.

"Well, maybe not quite that old. People didn't stay in school that long in those days. They had to work to help support their families. There was even a special school break in the fall so that everyone could help with the harvest. All of this land was farmland back then."

"So the bell had to be super loud, so they could hear it from across the fields?" Cam asked.

"I guess so!" their mom said with a laugh.

Hannah ran her hand over the dark wood of the door frame.

"Cam and me would have been in the same class here?"

"Well, not here, but over by North Plains."

"Why not here?" Hannah asked.

"Well, as far as I can tell, this is just a building done up to look like a pioneer school house. If you come over here..." Mom led them back into the hallway where the three old-time pictures hung on the wall. "This picture of the Leisyville school looks very similar to this building, but the very first

Jackson School House probably looked a lot more like one of these." She pointed to a set of pictures of short, stumpy log cabin schools. "It was torn down almost a hundred years ago. I'm not sure if they kept anything."

A little spark of anger settled in Hannah's chest. It only got bigger as she followed her mother around as she took pictures of this and

that and asked the office lady a few of her reporter questions.

Snowy still waited for them when they emerged from the fake school. They squatted around her and said hello. Clouds had darkened the neon sky. Hannah glanced up at them, scowling.

"What's the matter, Hannah-Bannah?" Mom asked.

"It's fake. AND they tore up the real one."

"Ah." Hannah could tell that her mother was itching to get back to work, but something made her change her mind. She sat down on the porch, and Hannah and her brother perched on either side.

They all watched the storm clouds drift toward the Hare Wood with dramatic billows and swirls.

"Are you afraid people will forget, Han?"

"Well, they smashed it up. How can people remember?"

"Yeah, what about all the kids that went to school there? That was their memories from when they were kids," Cam agreed.

"Exactly," Hannah said. "I always felt cozy there, because of their memories. But now I know it wasn't even real!"

Their mother nodded and was quiet for a while.

Finally, she looked up. "Maybe you can think of it like this: You know about old stories, stories like King Arthur? You know

LOOK UP AT THE BELL.

how they change over years and years? Every generation has different problems, different reasons they need those stories, so they change them to fit what they need them to do. Well, this new Jackson School House..." She stood up and walked with them down to the sidewalk, so they could turn and look at the building. "This new Jackson School House is the story that our generation needed, but in it is the memory of all those pioneer school houses that *were* real, that helped build our community and gave our children a chance to grow their minds and their friendships.

"When you look up at the bell, you remember those kids chatting as they hurried up the steps to whichever schoolhouse was theirs. When you look at the hitching post, you remember how far they had to come, just for the privilege of learning.

"Old stories, powerful stories, have a way of leaving memories behind in newer stories. They remind us that where we came from is also part of where we are. So in a way, what you felt was real. It was just even bigger than you thought."

A huge gust of wind whipped around them, pulling strands from their mother's heavy red braids and sending Hannah's short black curls flying. Shadows fell over the school house, taking away its bright newness, and suddenly, Hannah could see exactly what her mother meant.

The old memories.

In the new stories.

Hannah and Cam exchanged a look. The school house *was* kind of magical, if she thought about it that way. She smiled at her brother, knowing he was thinking the same thing.

Then Snowy, the last of their guards, began jumping against their calves and driving them toward home.

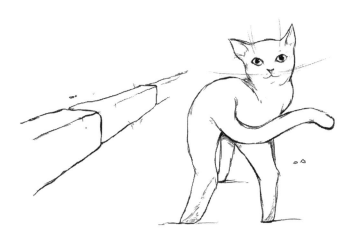

LOOKING A LITTLE CAT-LIKE.

Chapter Two

A Secret in the Blackberry Brambles

"Don't you dare bring those cat fur clothes in here!" Mom warned. "Change in the laundry room and leave them on the floor. When you are done, there are peanut butter and honey cups in the fridge. I've got to get to work. *Wash your hands!*"

Cam got to the laundry room first, leaving Hannah to wait at the stairs. She started to sit down, but her mom looked back with the evil eye and Hannah popped back up again. She looked down at her leggings. Whoa. When you petted every single cat in the entire neighborhood on the way home, pretty soon you started to look a little cat-like yourself, she guessed.

The office door slammed shut.

The laundry room door slammed open.

Cam bolted for the kitchen, starving as always. Hannah re-emerged from the laundry room, just in time to hear his upstairs bedroom door slam, too.

For a minute, she stood in the living room just staring at all the closed doors.

A hot, painful little squeeze worked its way into her throat.

"Stupid first day of summer vacation."

Her legs wanted to run back out the front door to the kitty honor guard and steal another snuggle, but she had to remind those itchy legs that the cats had disappeared just as strangely as they had appeared. It had been wonderful—and odd—but it was over.

She ran a hand over Nicola's empty kitty bed on the corner of the couch. The dried-up roses she and Cam had laid there for her funeral tumbled to the side. She set them right again.

"Bet you would have loved to see that, huh, little Nicola?"

Dropping her hand, Hannah trudged into the kitchen and pulled her PB and honey cup from the fridge. Mom had stood a bunch of carrot and celery sticks up in its creamy goodness and sprinkled chocolate chips around the edge for a treat. When Dad had been laid off two years ago, snacks stopped being wrapped in fancy plastic and foil. Dad had only found a job around St. Patrick's Day, so money still wasn't back up to plastic-wrapped snacks. Pretty early on, Hannah had decided she would trade granola bars and fruit gummies for keeping the house any day. And the nice thing about leggings? They could get a couple inches short and nobody cared.

She wandered to the window and looked out. Lion Kitty stood in his usual spot behind the fence, staring patiently into the blackberry brambles, his orange fur thick and tussled by the bushes and the breeze.

Hannah knew what he was looking at. And that was exactly where she wanted to be right now. If everyone else was going to ignore her, she would ignore them right back.

After a quick dash up to her room to get her art bag, Hannah pushed out of the back door and out into the stormy afternoon air. For a second, she crunched her carrots and closed her eyes, listening to the wind toss the tree branches, feeling the silky toss of her curls against her face.

She knew that the narrow nature preserve behind her house had once been the big, beautiful Hare Wood, owned by the Hare family, one of the "early families"—as her mother called them—that had helped Hillsboro turn into a real town. That knowledge always made her feel a little guilty that big trees had died to make space for the house she lived in, the house her parents worked so hard to keep safe from the bank.

The Hares' family home had been torn down, their woods ripped away, but Hannah still thought she could feel something ancient there, something older than the Hare family, even older than the Atfalati tribe that had sometimes wandered through here in the days before the pioneers. So when Lion Kitty had shown her the entrance to the blackberry brambles, she knew this was where she wanted to make her home.

"I need my wishing stone," she muttered, wandering through the tangley plants of the backyard, looking for rocks. At the base of the bleeding heart, something shiny caught her eye. Digging into the dirt, she worked free a little chunk of quartz with green lace inside.

She rubbed it clean on her shorts and then tested the feel of it in her hand.

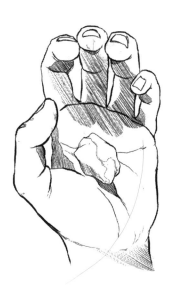

"Perfect."

Quietly, as not to disturb Lion Kitty, Hannah slipped

BETWEEN THE STUMP AND THE BLACKBERRIES.

through the back gate, careful not to let the grabby claws of the blackberry bushes catch at her.

"Hello, sir," she said, trying to give Lion Kitty plenty of warning. This time, though, he didn't move as Hannah crouched beside him. Here between the mossy stump and the clawed arms of the blackberry brambles lay the entrance to her home. Here was the place where a family that was too busy and friends who never wanted to play didn't matter. Here she didn't have to argue with anyone or play stupid games or do chores. She could just sit and draw and think until she was done. And Lion Kitty would stand guard at the door to keep her safe.

After a couple of quick snips at the blackberry runners with her dad's gardening shears—stolen from his tools months ago—she crawled inside her little bower.

HER HIDEAWAY WAS PERFECT.

Chapter Three

A Mysterious Invader

Hannah settled in her small bower with her back against the crumbling stump, dug into her art bag, and pulled out a flashlight. Her hideaway was perfect in so many ways, small, dark, cozy. It had only two problems: the snakes and the spiders that sometimes also liked to hide here, and the weirdoes who sometimes hung out in the woods behind it. For the snakes and the spiders, she had a jar and a stick. For the weirdoes, she turned off the flashlight and froze like a statue. She rubbed at the blackberry scratch on her arm. The weirdoes probably couldn't get through the brambles from that side. She'd only seen two so far this year, but it still creeped her out.

Hannah took a deep breath and flipped on the flashlight. Inch-by-inch she searched the woven branches for eight-legged friends. She knocked one into her jar; the other one got

away. No snakes this time. The snakes learned faster than the spiders.

Hannah twisted around to inspect her seat on the stump. She froze. Cautiously, she set down her jar and her stick and turned around on her toes.

"Someone has been in here!"

On the sides of the little seat she had chipped out of the stump, someone had tied two bouquets of bright red poppies. Gingerly, she touched the fuzzy, prickly stems.

"He does NOT get to come in here! This is MY place!"

She reached out to rip the flowers down, then snatched her hand back. What if it wasn't Cam who had put them in here? What if Diana or Clark put them in here? Did they

HE DOES NOT GET TO COME IN HERE!

know about her secret place? What if it wasn't any of them? What if it was one of the weirdoes? What if one of them had seen her in here? These flowers weren't wilty from the ninety-five-degree heat this morning before the storm had started drifting down the hills.

Hannah pushed a hand against her chest to shush her fast-beating heart. She took off her art bag, switched off her flashlight, and covered up the last of her PB and honey. She would go and she would ask. Sitting here and being scared was silly. This was her special place. She wasn't going to let it be ruined like this. Maybe her friends just meant it as a gift.

Maybe that was all it was: a gift.

Because her brother Cam sure as heck wouldn't put flowers in here!

Hannah pushed her way back out of the bower. She came nose to whiskers with Lion Kitty. He was not pleased.

"Merrow!"

"I'll be right back. I just need to check and make sure. Excuse me!"

Lion Kitty did not move. Hannah ground her teeth in frustration. She knew Lion Kitty

didn't like to be petted, and she was trying to be nice, but...

"Excuse me, Lion Kitty. I am getting out!"

The huge orange tom sat down and stared back at her, totally offended.

"Seriously?! Well, keep your claws to yourself, Mister, 'cause you are not keeping me in here." And with that fair warning, she pushed herself out right over the top of him.

"Merrow!" he scolded.

"I'll just be a second," she replied, squeezing her back where the blackberries had gotten her.

Mindful of the tiny creatures who would be after her PB and honey and the ring of chocolate chips she had saved for last, Hannah hurried through the neighbors' back gate and up to their sliding-glass back door. She saw Diana and Clark wandering through the living room and dining room, calling for Bruce, their kitty. She had a bad feeling Bruce wasn't in the house to answer. He'd been in the after-school honor guard.

"Uh-oh," she whispered to herself, the guilty feeling coming back.

Biting her lip, she rapped on the door.

Clark ran over to open it. Clark Talwar was a year older than her; Diana Talwar was a year older than Cameron—she would be the first of them to head off to middle school next year. Diana always wore glasses and a bun just like Wonder Woman when she was pretending to be a regular person. Clark wore his hair gelled and spiky and was way better looking than Superman when he was pretending to be a regular person. Not that that was the reason she got nervous whenever he was around. She could still nail him with a water gun, if she had to.

"What's going on, Han-Stan? We're kinda busy right now."

Hannah stopped herself from scowling at him. Did everybody have to have a stupid rhyme for her name?

"I just had a question: Have you guys been back in the woods today?"

"Dude, we've been in school and then we came home to find out Bruce has disappeared."

"Children, do not hold the door open," Apsara hollered at them from the kitchen.

"Hannah, please come inside. We cannot find our cat. Perhaps you have seen him?"

As ordered, Hannah stepped inside and peered around herself for the millionth time at Diana and Clark's dad's ever-growing collection of superhero pictures and statues and stuff. Her own mom couldn't believe Apsara let Ravi plaster the house with that junk. Her own dad couldn't believe Apsara let Ravi name their kids after action figures. Hannah just thought it was cool. She spotted a new Wonder Woman pencil drawing on the wall next to her and wandered over to it to study the shading.

"Um," she paused in answering Apsara's question, wondering how ridiculous the kitty honor guard would sound to somebody who

BRUCE HAS DISAPPEARED.

hadn't seen it. Grown-ups had a funny way of thinking you were lying, if things didn't sound just right to their ears.

Suddenly, the most horrible screech came from the back door where she had just been standing. All four of them ran to the door.

There was Bruce, his lean, solid black body pacing back and forth in front of the door. He

raised up on his back legs and ran his claws down the glass.

SCREEEEECH!

Clark unlocked the door. Bruce bounded straight for Hannah and let out the worst caterwaul she had ever heard. Hannah clapped her hands over her ears and squeezed her eyes shut. The scream ended and Hannah carefully peeked down at him.

"Holy cow, Bruce! Be nice!" Diana said, reaching for him.

Bruce dodged her grasp and Diana tumbled into her mother. Hannah turned with the cat and found herself being backed toward the open door. She caught the door frame as she stepped down to the porch. Bruce stopped at the doorway.

"Perrow," he said, this time with a much gentler voice.

"Perrow to you, too," Hannah replied.

"Hannah, I am so sorry for our cat's very poor manners!" Again, Apsara looked appalled.

Hannah just shook her head. She reached down and let Bruce sniff her hand. He gave her hand a little head butt and she scratched him behind the ear.

"It's all right," she said. "He just knows I have somewhere I need to go. See you guys later!"

Diana succeeded in scooping up her cat this time and held him tight, looking strangely like her mother during the purse episode after school. Clark stood holding the door and looked at her funny. What could she possibly say? He couldn't know how completely weird her day had already been.

So Hannah just smiled at him.

And left to keep her promise.

THE QUARTZ GLOWED LIKE SOMETHING MAGICAL.

Chapter Four

THE SHRIEKING WOOD

Hannah's wishing stone poked her thigh as she crawled back into her bower—this time with Lion Kitty's permission.

"I forgot to add it to my pattern," she told him.

Awkwardly, she wrestled it from her pocket. She found her flashlight and flipped it back on. Settling back on her stump chair, she checked her PB and honey for ants, then scooped up the last of it with the crunchy, rich chocolate chips.

"Yum!"

Hannah held the stone up to the light of her flashlight. The quartz glowed like something magical with its swirls of green.

"I'll add you to the wave," she decided.

She turned the flashlight to the floor of her bower. She had built it one stone at a time, trying to copy a picture she'd seen of a pebble mosaic in Greece with ocean waves on the edges and diamonds in the middle. She was nearly half done.

Or at least she had been.

Someone had pulled up every last pebble.

And had started building a picture of their own.

A tear splashed on Hannah's cheek. All of her work. All of her months and months of work. It wasn't bad enough that someone had invaded her secret place. Oh, no. No, they had to destroy her pebble picture, too.

"No, no, no, NO!"

She clawed at the ground, ripping at her wishing stones, digging them from the damp soil, between sniffles.

"Why would you do this? This isn't yours! I hate you!"

She piled the small stones between her feet as she grabbed more and more bits of quartz and jasper and obsidian and even just plain orbs of river rock that had once felt so comforting to her hand. Around her the brambles shook. With each rock that she took back, the shaking became more violent—just like her anger.

Once she had raked up every rock she could find, she reached behind herself and ripped away the bundles of poppies and threw them out. Lion Kitty ducked to the side.

Abruptly, the shaking stopped.

Hannah froze.

Outside she heard the thunder crack. Lightning flashed, lighting up the spaces the flashlight couldn't fill.

He was staring at her.

She stared back, frozen.

He hunched about ten feet away on the other side of the brambles, peering at her through the criss-crosses of vines. She knew his face: long, bony with a ratty beard and crazy eyes. She'd seen him before in the Hare Wood, watched him silently from her hiding place. He had never seen her.

He saw her now.

He grinned, his teeth crooked and yellow against his too-large blue bathrobe.

"So that's where you've been hiding, little girl, little girl. Our little Dolasílla. Did you dream well with the stone you stole from me, little Dolasílla?"

The wishing stones in Hannah's hands grew suddenly warm in her muddy palms.

Blue Bathrobe Man cocked his head to the side. "Have you forgotten, Dolasílla?

"Clang, clang, clang:
The sword against the golden gate.
The treasure waits within.
One treasure brings one heart true love;
One treasure brings the world to end.

"Clang, clang, clang:
The sword against the sword.

SO THAT'S WHERE YOU'VE BEEN HIDING.

The guide waits within.
The mother brings the marmot peace;
The father brings the eagle war.

"Clang, clang, clang:
The arrow against the shield.
The hero waits within.
The eye of night brings tired-heart peace;
The warrior brings red poppy dreams.

"Clang, clang, clang:
The sword against the stone.
The traitor waits within.
The king brings greed's final betrayal;
The prince brings pride's final blow.

"Clang, clang, clang:
The trumpet against the bone.

The promise waits within.
The queen brings one eternal hope;
The Fànes will rise once more!"

With each part of his rhyme, Blue Bathrobe Man's voice grew wilder. The storm wind whipped his greasy hair and thrashed the tree branches until they creaked. Hannah clutched her art bag to her chest.

Then she realized the creaking sound she heard wasn't creaking after all.

Blue Bathrobe Man realized this, too, and looked up.

Hannah recognized the shriek of angry squirrels. The Hare Wood filled with squirrel voices, so loud, so shrill, she had to cover her ears. Blue Bathrobe Man ducked away from the sound and disappeared from her view.

OH, MY CREEPING CATERPILLARS, HANNAH!

Hannah didn't hesitate. Grabbing her art bag, she burst out of her bower and ran.

Lion Kitty was gone.

She saw Cam and Mom on the back porch, calling for her. She ran to her mother and grabbed her arm.

"Oh, my creeping caterpillars, Hannah! What happened to you?" her mother yelled over the screams of the squirrels.

Hannah pulled on her mother's arm and grabbed her brother.

"There's a bad guy in the woods! Come on! Come on!"

She dragged them into the house and slammed the door behind them.

THE SQUIRRELS ARE SCREAMING.

Chapter Five

WHO REALLY WANTS TO BE ORDINARY?

"**I don't know.** The squirrels are screaming like the Vikings are invading. Could it be a cougar? Wasn't there a cougar sighting at Jackson Bottom last summer?"

Hannah waited quietly at the dinner table, her eyes trained on the storm-tossed trees, her ears trained on the reply from the police woman answering her mother on the phone. She couldn't quite understand what the police woman said, but from the way her mother said "oh," she could guess that screaming wasn't a normal squirrel reaction to cougars.

Besides, Hannah was pretty sure she knew who the squirrels were screaming at.

And last time she checked, cougars didn't wear blue bathrobes.

Hannah shifted her grip on the pencil she held pressed to her drawing notebook. Just that little shift of her T-shirt smeared more anti-bacterial cream across her back and shoulders and made the T-shirt fabric stick to her skin. Her blackberry scratches were not amused. She twisted her face at the pain. Pulling her gaze from the big picture window framing the Hare Wood, Hannah turned her attention back to her drawing.

She began adding the details: the twists of his greasy hair, the shading that made the deep hollows of his cheeks. She drew in the torn seam at the shoulder of his robe. The eyes weren't right. She went after them with her eraser and her lead, making them wider, wilder.

She stared at the picture.

Clang, clang, clang:

The sword against the golden gate.

She couldn't remember the whole chant, not precisely, but the words tickled around in the dark caverns of her mind where forgotten things hid. She couldn't stop thinking about it, just a little afraid of what forgotten things might come out of those dark caves if she kept poking at the memory.

Cameron came rumbling down the stairs. He ran to the back door, his remote control spy car in hand. The second he laid his hand on the dead-bolt, Mom interrupted her conversation with the police woman.

"Don't you dare go out there."

Cameron raised the car in her direction, then unlocked the door, set the car outside, and closed the door again, locking it. Mom

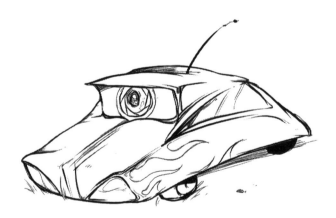

nodded in understanding as Cam used his video remote to drive the car toward the back garden gate. Hannah had never understood why the toy was called a spy car. Sure, it could take secret videos, but driving it made more noise than the screaming squirrels.

"Can you at least send someone to take a look in the woods? That man shook my daughter up pretty badly."

More like the man had shaken *Mom* up pretty badly.

Hannah traded her pencil for the cup of hot cocoa in front of her. Hot cocoa on the first day of summer break? It could almost top the kitty honor guard and screaming squirrels outside.

Her mom's pacing had moved from the kitchen area to the dining room. She stopped next to Hannah, reached over her shoulder and spun the sketch of Blue Bathrobe Man to face her.

"Yeah, my daughter has a pretty good sketch of the guy, if your people want to take a look at it. All right. We'll wait for your call."

Mom flicked off her phone and tossed it on the table.

"They're sending someone to check out the woods. They're going to give us a call when they're done," she reported.

Hannah nodded.

"I can't get my car through the blackberry bushes," Cam complained.

MY DAUGHTER HAS A PRETTY GOOD SKETCH.

"I'm pretty sure the raccoon family has a path that comes out by the wisteria," Hannah offered.

She stood up with her cocoa and walked around the table to the window, pulling her T-shirt away from the slime on her back. She leaned against the window sill. Pretty soon her mom and brother were standing next to her.

Clang, clang, clang:

The arrow against the shield.

The hero waits within.

Hannah rubbed her fingers against her temple and took another sip of her cocoa. The storm made the trees of the Hare Wood dance wildly, even dangerously—all three of them eyed Big Ben warily. Before the destruction, when Hare Wood had been a big, beautiful forest, the smaller trees around the edges had provided protection against the wind for the spindly, taller fir trees at the center. Now Big Ben creaked and bled

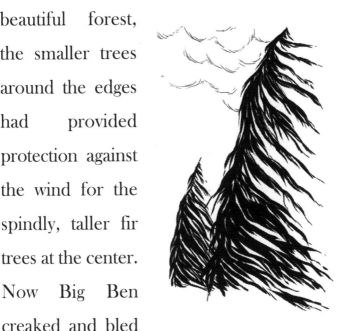

in the storm winds that came over the hills from the ocean.

"Just let him fall the other way when he goes," her mother murmured into her own cocoa.

"Yeah," Cameron agreed.

"That's what happens when you chop the old places down," Hannah said.

Her mother chuckled. "And just where would you propose all these people live?" she asked, gesturing toward their neighbors. "Things have to change sooner or later. There's no stopping that."

Hannah frowned. "Yeah, I know, but...but don't you think that a lot of times when they change, they get less... less..." She flailed her hand around, not coming up with the right word.

"Maybe just...less?" Cam suggested. "I kinda get what you mean. It's hard for kids like us to picture this whole huge neighborhood belonging to just one family. It's hard to imagine the woods without bike trails and graffiti. It just seems like back then it was 'more.'"

"That's totally what I mean," Hannah agreed. "The forest was more magical, because people hadn't ripped it all up and there was more space for people to do amazing things, 'cause there weren't so many people around. When you and the neighbor guy, Trevor, were talking, you said that John D. Hare was an Oregon congressman and a senator. He did big things. He could be special."

He could be a hero. Just like in the poem.

When their mother laughed, she sounded a little sad. Hannah knew then that her mother and brother understood the weird, achy longing in her chest.

"Yeah," her mother murmured. "Sometimes it seems like the world was big enough for heroes back then. And now it is all chopped up into tiny little pieces. Too many people, too little room for anyone to be somebody special anymore. There's an old saying, 'When everybody's special, nobody's special.' But who really wants to be ordinary?"

"Apparently not us," Cam joked, and they all chuckled.

"Well, there was certainly nothing ordinary about today," their mother agreed.

"No kidding," Hannah said, the smile returning to her face.

The doorbell rang.

BUT WHO REALLY WANTS TO BE ORDINARY?

Mom set down her mug on the table behind her, grabbed Hannah's drawing, and trotted off to answer the door.

"I really need to call your father after this!"

Hannah and Cam hung back a bit as Mom talked to two officers so packed with equipment and safety gear that they couldn't put their arms down at their sides.

"We came in from opposite ends of the woods, but we didn't see anyone back there, ma'am," the shorter one told them.

"Those squirrels, though, if anyone had been back there, they'd have cleared out long before we got there. I had my earplugs in the whole time I was back there and my ears are still ringing," the taller officer said, rubbing at her ears.

"Sorry we couldn't be more help tonight, but be sure to call us right away if you see him again."

The short officer took a picture of Hannah's drawing with her phone and they said goodnight. Hannah, Cameron, and their mother watched the door close.

"I don't feel better," Hannah said.

Cameron draped an arm over her shoulder. Mom walked over and wrapped them both in a tight hug.

"Me either, Hannah-Bannah. Guess we'll be using nightlights tonight won't we?"

Hannah didn't answer, but just snuggled closer in with her brother and mother.

HANNAH STARED AT THE CURTAINS IN THE DARK.

Chapter Six

OTHER USES FOR A SCHOOL BELL

Hannah sat in her bed and stared at the curtains in the dark. The squirrels had stopped screaming, but now the wind was blowing so hard that their mom had unplugged all the computers before she sent them to bed—just in case the power went out.

"If Big Ben makes it through this, I will be really impressed," she'd told them. "Somebody's going to fall tonight. That's for sure."

Hannah could hear her mom talking to their dad on the phone. He was in Ireland this week, not quite close enough to visit his parents back in Italy, but way too far away from his family.

Especially tonight.

Hannah finally gave up. She slid out of bed and out of her room. She knocked quietly on Cam's door.

After a few seconds she heard him thump to the floor and pad over to the door. He poked his head out. His hair stuck out in big cowlicks.

"I can't sleep," she whispered.

"Yeah, me neither."

"Can you come sleep in my room?" she asked.

"You ask Mom?"

"She's on the phone with Dad. Can you just bring your mattress in my room?"

Cam thought for a second, then nodded. "Sure."

As quietly as they could, they tipped Cam's mattress off his bed and slid it on its side into the hallway. Then they pushed it back through Hannah's doorway. Hannah looked around

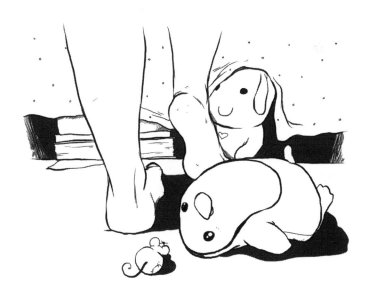

at all the shadows on her floor. Quickly, she kicked piles of stuffies out of the way and pushed a stack of books under the bed with her other foot. They let the mattress tip over. Cam went back to his room for his bedding and pillow...and his wand.

His wand was from an old birthday party, made of a wooden chopstick with a hilt of thick glue painted gold and embedded with jewels. He slept with it under his pillow every night.

Hannah climbed back into her bed and pushed the curtains open while Cam re-created his nest of blankets and sheets.

"I think we're actually going to get some more lightning," she told her brother.

Cam climbed up on her bed and peered out with her at the shimmering clouds.

"Crazy," he agreed.

Just then the first boom of thunder shook the window under their hands.

They both jumped.

"See," she bragged to her brother. "I can tell the future."

They laughed nervously.

"I feel like those kids in that story Mom read us from the old Hillsboro newspaper. You know the ones who had to hide in the hayloft from the Native Americans while their mom went off to help sick people?" Hannah whispered, settling her chin on the sill and peeking out over the empty street below.

"Eliza Williams, the nurse? Yeah, they were either really brave or she was really crazy," Cam said, settling his chin on the sill, too. "But, she did have them pull the ladder up. And she did say the Native Americans really only stole things they could reach from the windows. They were pretty desperate."

"I think you had to be way braver in those days. There's no way I could sleep like that. I would be thinking of all the ways the bad guys could climb up to get me!" Hannah turned to flop on her bed.

"You mean kinda like now?" Cam teased.

"Exactly."

Cam climbed over her and down to his own mattress. Hannah tucked under her covers and hugged them to her chin.

The thunder boomed again.

Hannah covered her ears with her blanket.

"Holy cow! There's no way I can sleep through this!"

"You've got to try," Cam told her. "Want to borrow my wand?"

"Does that really help you sleep?"

"Well, yeah. I put my hand on it and it makes me think of magical things instead of

stupid things that happened during the day."
Cam's arm appeared over the side of the bed,
holding the wand up to her.

She pushed it back down. "It's okay.
Maybe I'll try my dream stone."

Hannah sat up and opened the drawer to
her nightstand. After a little feeling around,
she found the large smooth piece of agate that
she'd gotten from the Rice Rock & Mineral
Museum. Wrapping her hand securely
around it, she tucked it under her pillow
beneath her cheek.

"Goodnight."

"Goodnight," Cam replied drowsily.

Hannah closed her eyes. She thought of
magical things. She thought of fairies with
glittering wings and unicorns with silken

I'LL TRY MY DREAM STONE.

manes and waterfalls with secret caves. She thought of wishing stones, plucked from a garden, arranged in a lovely pattern on the floor of her bower. And the evil person who had destroyed her sacred, secret place.

She tossed in her bed with a cry of frustration.

Lightning lit up the room and she squeezed her eyes

tight, determined to try again. She rubbed the stone with her thumb. Magical things. Brownies in the woods, hiding behind the leaves, dancing in the—

Thunder shook the house.

Hannah jumped.

She heard a familiar whine. She opened her eyes. The streetlight was out. So was her alarm clock.

"Whoa," Cam said, sitting up.

Hannah sat up, too, her heart pounding. The lightning came again and again, one flash right after the other. And the rain started.

"What's that sound?" Cam asked.

Hannah leaned over the bed. "What sound?"

"That sound. The dong, dong, dong."

Hannah held still and listened.

"It's a bell," she said, finally hearing it. It was getting louder and louder.

"But none of the churches around here have bells," Cam protested.

He climbed back up onto Hannah's bed and they clung to the windowsill, staring out into the very dark night. He reached over and cracked the window.

Dong, dong, dong.

Clang, clang, clang!

Hannah's chest tightened. She turned to stare at Cam.

"That's not a church bell. That's the school bell. The bell from the Jackson School House."

"It's so loud!" Cam shouted, reaching for the window.

But just as he did, another flash of lightning flared across the cloudy sky.

Hannah jumped to her feet, grabbing at her brother.

There in the center of the street stood Blue Bathrobe Man, his tattered robe soaked and flapping, his wild eyes staring up at her bedroom window.

"It's him! It's him!"

Cam froze and stared. Hannah watched, waiting for the lightning to flash again, just to be sure.

There he was.

But something was wrong with his face. It was white and shiny. No, Hannah realized, it

IT'S HIM! IT'S HIM!

wasn't a face at all: his head had become a long skull, like a horse, or a donkey, or a mule.

Cam slammed the window shut.

"Mom!" they screamed.

They scrambled off the bed to another flash of lightning.

They grabbed each other just as they were about to jump from Cam's mattress to the floor.

Lion Kitty sat with his thick tail flicking impatiently...in front of Hannah's closed bedroom door.

"PERROW!"

LION KITTY YOWLED AGAIN.

Chapter Seven

A Trail of Muddy Paw Prints

"Ooookay," Hannah said, trying to catch her balance.

"Perrow!" Lion Kitty yowled again.

"But how did he get in here?" Cam demanded, stepping off of the mattress. Hannah followed.

Lion Kitty began to circle them, leaping first to Hannah's reading chair, then to Cam's mattress, leaving a trail of muddy paw prints and yowling over the noise of the storm.

Hannah knew this dance. Bruce had done the same thing back at Diana and Clark's house.

"He wants us to go somewhere," she told her brother.

"I figured that out. We need to get Mom. Come on."

Cam led the way out the door.

Lion Kitty drove them straight to their parents' room down the hall. They burst into the room. Their mom stopped in the middle of pulling clothes out of the closet.

"What's the matter? The storm—"

"Mom! The guy is in front of the house!" Hannah shouted.

"He is! I saw him, too!" Cam said, grabbing their mother's arm.

"Yeah, and he's got a skull head. And Lion Kitty's in the house!"

Their mother stared at them sternly. Then Lion Kitty came into the room, leaving muddy tracks on their dad's grandma's rug.

"Oh, my mopping mice, how did he get in here. Out, out!" But Mom went back to the closet and grabbed her bad guy bat as she followed them out the door. "Show me," she ordered.

Together they crossed back to Hannah's window and looked out over the street below. On went the lightning like a stage light; Blue Bathrobe Man stood at its center, a soggy scarecrow in a black field, first with a man's head, then with a horse's skull.

He began moving toward the house.

LION KITTY GRABBED HANNAH'S PAJAMAS.

"That's not good," Mom muttered.

"Perrow!" Lion Kitty began butting against Hannah's thigh.

"Is that the old school house bell?" Mom asked as she pulled both Hannah and Cam from the bed.

"Yeah," Hannah answered. "We think so. It's a warning bell, isn't it?"

Mom tried to drag them toward her bedroom, but Lion Kitty grabbed Hannah's pajama pants and pulled hard, nearly knocking her over. Hannah opened her mouth to scold the cat, but after a second, she closed it again and turned to her mom instead.

"Mom, I think we need to get out of here. Right now."

"What? Out there? I don't—"

Lion Kitty yanked Hannah toward the stairs.

"Mom, the kitty guard, the visit to the school house, the warning bell? Lion Kitty in my room when the door was closed? Do we need more weird to get the idea?" Hannah pointed to the cat keeping her foot off the floor by his teeth. "We need to get out of here!"

Hannah watched her mom's face. For all that her mother talked about old memories and new stories, it looked like her practical brain was going to win. Hannah stopped resisting the tug at her leg and followed Lion Kitty at a run down the stairs.

"Oh, fish fingers. Hannah, don't you—" Mom started, but then Hannah heard Cam come running after her. "At least get shoes and a jacket...and a flashlight!"

Hannah and Cam stopped long enough to cram their feet into sneakers. They grabbed their rain jackets from the closet. Lion Kitty was headed to the back door just as the front door began to rattle ever so slightly.

"Mom!" Cam shouted.

Mom came running down the stairs with a giant metal flashlight, the bad guy bat, and her cell phone. She pushed her feet into the boots Hannah held out for her. Cam

helped her pull on her rain jacket while they all stared at the front door. None of them was brave enough to put their eye to the peep hole.

"Perrow!"

"We're coming," Hannah called.

Pulling on their hoods, they all three dashed for the back door.

Lion Kitty led the way out into the rain. Mom trained the flashlight on the big tom cat as he ran. Hannah had a good idea where he was leading them.

There was no way they would all fit in her tiny little bower.

Mom's light hit the garden gate that led to the woods. Red poppies. The path from the garden gate to her bower was covered with big red poppies, bobbing in the rain. Hannah

PATH TO HER BOWER WAS COVERED IN POPPIES.

followed Lion Kitty into the tangled bed of flowers with Cam close behind her. Lion Kitty stepped to the side and Hannah did, too.

"Come on! Get inside," she told her mother and brother.

"What is this place?" Mom asked, helping Cam duck into the small entrance.

"My secret hiding place," Hannah said, pulling her mother's arm to get her to duck down. She was going to get so many scratches! She was too big!

"Nope, you first," Mom insisted.

Hannah started to protest, but quickly realized it would be faster just to go. She felt her mom shaking the vines right behind her.

To her surprise, they both fit easily inside with Cam.

"Lion Kitty, come on!"

Again to her surprise, he came when she called.

Mom trained her flashlight around the small cavern of branches. First on Hannah's seat with the new sets of poppies tied to either side of the throne. Then on the pebble floor made of wishing stones.

The floor was complete.

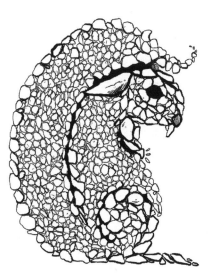

Hannah grabbed the flashlight from her mother and shined it on the mosaic.

"Move," she told her family as she

looked over the new image the stones made.

"You made this?" Mom asked.

"No, I didn't, but," she paused, looking down at the dream stone she still clutched in her hand, "I think I have the final piece. Don't I, Lion Kitty?"

Lion Kitty just looked up at her as the storm raged outside and the old school bell sang, "Clang, clang, clang!"

Everyone watched as Hannah slowly lowered her hand and placed the smooth piece of agate into the eye of the squirrel.

It fit perfectly.

The air around Hannah's body gave a little snap.

Then it became very still.

Hannah looked from her mother to her brother, each of them with their eyes wide. Something outside the bower crashed. Mom grabbed the flashlight and switched it off.

None of them moved.

The dark wrapped Hannah's senses in a thick, cold blanket of nothingness. She couldn't see either her brother or her mother and she had the panicked feeling that she was suddenly alone. Carefully, she reached out her hands toward them.

Her arm bumped their reaching hands and she could breathe again. They found each other's hands and squeezed tight.

"Look," their mother whispered, tugged down on Hannah's hand.

The dream stone, the eye of the squirrel, had begun to glow, sending tendrils of light swirling up from its center like the lace in the quartz she had found earlier this afternoon. The glow illuminated the serious face of Lion Kitty as he watched the light climb its own vines, growing, building.

Hannah glanced nervously toward the entrance of the bower. The light was getting so bright. Wouldn't Blue Bathrobe Man see it?

Lion Kitty circled the criss-crossing bars of light to Hannah's side. Soon Cam and Mom followed suit as the creation moved toward the forest-facing wall of the tiny hideaway. The glow became almost blinding, but Hannah stared as she saw what it had become: a gate.

"Clang, clang, clang:
The sword against the golden gate.
The treasure waits within.
One treasure brings one heart true love;
One treasure brings the world to end."

THE GOLDEN GATE SWUNG OPEN.

Cam looked at her curiously as she whispered the rhyme. Then Lion Kitty reared back and slammed his great forepaws forward.

The golden gate swung open.

HER HARE WOOD...AND YET NOT.

Chapter Eight

THE CONGRESS OF MARMOTS

On the other side of the gate, Hannah stretched herself upright. This was her Hare Wood...and yet not. The trees were not tagged with graffiti; blackberry brambles did not smother the undergrowth. Though she could still hear the midnight storm, in this narrow part of the woods, dim sunlight streamed through the branches to dance on the ferns at either side of a narrow path—almost like fairy light.

Hannah scooted out of Cam's way and saw Lion Kitty waiting at the bend in the path. Snowy sat regally beside him.

Mom finally pushed through the gate, then pulled it closed behind her. They all watched for just a moment to make sure it didn't disappear.

It didn't.

Hannah lifted a handful of threads from her mom's badly torn jacket. Her mom smiled.

"At least it's not pieces of me," she said with a grim chuckle. She nodded toward the path. "Your friends are leaving."

Hannah spun around just in time to see Snowy bounding down the path with Lion

Kitty right behind her. Hannah led the way after them.

She wasn't sure how far they'd run in this other Hare Wood, climbing over fallen trees and picking through scraggly overgrowth, but suddenly the cats came to a stop at a semi-circle of trees that glowed in the fairy light.

Hannah stopped watching her feet and looked up. Row after row of squirrels lined the five trees. She could hear the restless scratching of their claws as they repositioned themselves to watch her and her family. At their center, perched on a stump, two large squirrels stood, hands neatly folded against their round little bellies. One was as white as Snowy. The other was an earthy red, her head the color of granite. The cats bowed.

WELCOME, HANNAH, CAMERON, AND BRIDGET.

Startled, Hannah looked back to her mother and brother, who looked just as surprised as she was. Quickly, she did a short bow herself.

"Welcome, Hannah, Cameron, and Bridget Troyer," the red and gray squirrel said in a voice that came from her mouth and yet did not. The accent was strange and beautiful...and just a little bit familiar.

"Uh, hi," Hannah answered since she was in front.

"We of The Congress of Marmots greet you. We greet you and lament that Spina de Mùl has found you too soon. He has not forgotten his hatred of your people, but you have forgotten how to defend them. Most unfortunate. Most terribly unfortunate."

Talking squirrels. Hannah blinked. Twice.

Cameron stepped up beside her. Their mother closed up the circle, taking each of them by the shoulder and pulling them against her.

"Spinning Mule?" Cam asked. Hannah cringed, knowing he wasn't even close.

The white squirrel turned her head slowly toward him with her black-eyed stare. "The great sorcerer Spina de Mùl, he who can hide himself in the guise of a mule skeleton; he who cannot be killed by the cold metal of a blade. He knows his blood, his story. Do you?"

"Which story?" Mom asked cautiously, pulling Hannah and her brother in tighter.

But Hannah knew which story. She repeated lines that had been stuck in her head all night:

"Clang, clang, clang:
The sword against the golden gate.
The treasure waits within.
One treasure brings one heart true love;
One treasure brings the world to end."

In the storm beyond the fairy light, Hannah could still hear the school bell tolling. She watched the two squirrels on the stump. They did not reply.

"But how is this our story?" she asked. "I only heard it for the first time tonight."

The squirrels looked to each other.

"They no longer observe the spinwatch," the red-grey squirrel said mournfully. "They no longer tell the stories around the fire."

"And your father? He does not tell the stories?" the white squirrel asked, turning to Hannah.

"Our dad is an engineer. He reads us books sometimes, but mostly he works on his computer and travels to other countries

to teach other engineers," Cam replied.

The trees full of squirrels became silent and still.

"We dare not keep them in the

Between long enough for a full telling," murmured the red-grey squirrel. Then she straightened. "I will tell you what I can, what you *must* know. The rest you will have to discover for yourselves.

"In the days of copper and stone, there lived high up in the Dolomite mountains a people called the Fànes."

Hannah remembered the last line of the poem:

"The queen brings
one eternal hope;
The Fànes will rise
once more!"

She said it aloud and the white squirrel nodded, continuing the story: "In the beginning they were a peaceful people, protected by our great cousins, the marmots. Their last queen would marry a foreign prince to strengthen their kingdom and help ensure this peace."

The red-grey squirrel put a delicate paw on the arm of the smaller squirrel. The white squirrel lowered her head and the other, larger squirrel continued the story. "But the queen made a terrible mistake. She married a prince who was proud, greedy, and foolish. They had two daughters, Dolasílla and Luyànta. Luyànta went to live with the marmots to learn their peaceful ways, but Dolasílla stayed with her greedy father who chose instead to ally himself

TWO DAUGHTERS, DOLASÍLLA AND LUJÀNTA.

with the King of the Fire Eagles. Through dwarf magic, she became an archer, the leader of his army, conquering kingdom after kingdom.

"Spina de Mùl had little difficulty gathering the king's enemies against the Fànes; he had even less trouble wooing that greedy king's heart with tales of the treasures of the Auròna—beyond the lost golden gate to that underground kingdom.

"Dolasílla could not hold off such a great force, not when betrayed by her father, the king, in exchange for the location of the golden gate. She fell in battle. Spina de Mùl reclaimed the Rayéta Stone from her gleaming crown, and her people were forced to hide in the caves and warrens of their former protectors, the marmots."

The red-grey squirrel sounded so sad, so tired. Hannah's heart ached for her, but at the same time a chill shivered through her chest. Dolasílla fell in battle. Spina de Mùl had called *her* Dolasílla.

"There were so few of us left, but we negotiated peace. We would have been done with war. But then the traitor king's son, the Eagle Prince, returned, and his pride and his greed were as great as his father's. We were destroyed," the white squirrel finished.

The red-grey squirrel drew herself up regally and leveled her black eyes directly at Hannah. "The silver trumpets sounded year after year; the King of the Fire Eagles lit the bonfires in remembrance of the Fànes' great kingdom. On the appointed night each year, the queen and the marmot princess sailed the lake, waiting for the son of the Eagle Prince to return with Dolasílla's unfailing arrows and restore their people.

"He never came.

"And now the queen lies in rest at the bottom of the lake. She lies waiting until the

promised time shall come when she shall lead her people into a time of peace once more."

As the red-grey squirrel queen finished speaking, one by one, The Congress of Marmots began slipping from the trees, from branch to branch or across the forest floor. At Hannah's feet, Lion Kitty and Snowy began pacing restlessly.

"The time has come for you to return," the white squirrel princess said.

"Spina de Mùl called me Dolasílla. What does that mean?"

"You carry your people's blood in your veins, young Hannah. The fate of the kingdom depends on your courage, your wisdom...your heart."

"But I'm just a kid!"

"So was Dolasílla."

The fairy light began to shimmer. A drop of rain hit Hannah's cheek. Both she and Cam looked up.

"We'd better get out of here," Cam said, and Hannah knew he was right.

"I don't understand. What are we supposed to do?" their mother asked the two remaining squirrels, even as she dragged Cam and Hannah in the direction Lion Kitty and Snowy led.

The squirrels didn't answer.

Hannah didn't remember returning through the golden gate.

Or crawling through her bower.

But she stood now with her brother and mother at the entrance to her hideaway where the strange bed of red poppies had stood. In their place was black ash—like the remains of a fire that had burned nothing but the tangle of flowers themselves.

Hannah slipped her hands into the safety of her brother and mother's larger ones. They

THE MAGIC IS REAL!

watched together as the brilliant colors of morning cleared the storm clouds away.

They'd been gone longer than she'd thought.

She'd never seen such a huge display at sunrise. She knew this was the beginning of something even bigger. Her heart didn't know what to feel. Her mind didn't know what to think.

Beside her Cam kicked at a lump of ash.

"It's like their magic was used up," he murmured. Then he turned his head to the side and grinned at Hannah. "Hey, Han. The magic is real!"

Hannah look from his grin to her mother's weird expression and then back again.

"Yeah," she said. "I guess it is."

"That is so cool!" Cam exclaimed as he ran for the door.

Laughing, she chased after him.

"Don't you wear those ash-covered shoes into the house!" their mother shouted after them.

But she was laughing, too.

The End
Book One

Meet the Author!

Tonya Macalino

lives in that space Between—where the crossroads of past and present tease the senses, taunt the almost-memory. Haunted by story, she seeks it in the shadowy landscapes of history and in the blinding glare of what-may-come, both alone and with her family of children's book authors: Raymond, Damien, & Heléna Macalino.

Need another glimpse behind the veil? Subscribe to Tonya's Reader Group at www.tonyamacalino.com for free books, guides, videos, and more! You can also drop by and chat with her on Facebook at www.facebook.com/TonyaMacalino or on Twitter @TonyaMacalino.

Got grown-ups?

Send them to Tonya's website to learn more about her national award-winning supernatural thrillers for adults, SPECTRE OF INTENTION and THE SHADES OF VENICE series!

MEET THE ARTIST!

Maya Lilova

is a humble illustrator from Sofia, Bulgaria who loves reading—and drawing—a good story. You can find her at www.mayalilova.com for an assortment of artwork or on www.facebook.com/scruffydays for a friendly chat.

Hannah and Cameron's adventure is just beginning

and so is yours!

A glimpse into the future...

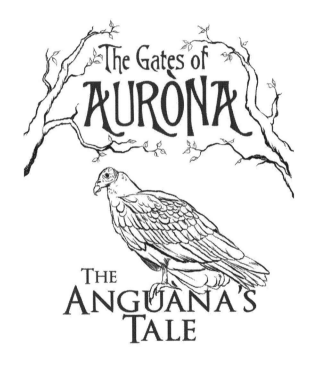

Coming Spring 2017

Chapter One

REALITY IN RUINS

Hannah Troyer rolled the last disk of hot dog around the bottom of what had been a heaping bowl of mac and cheese. The big picture window at the end of the table had her, her brother, Cameron, and her mother, Bridget, silent and transfixed. After so many years of waiting, Big Ben, the tallest, spindliest fir tree in the Hare Wood had fallen.

Not far, thank goodness.

No, his brother and sister trees had caught him—for now.

But the roar and snarl of chainsaws ripped apart the peace after last night's storm and Big Ben's bleeding peak shook with his final moments. Hannah's tummy turned sour over her last bite of lunch and she put her spoon down. Suddenly, Big Ben stopped shaking. The chainsaws fell silent. Mom reached over and put her hand over Hannah's.

Big Ben fell straight down through the arms of his sisters and brothers.

"I guess Spinning Mule got somebody last night after all," Cam said.

Mom reached across the table and put her other hand over Cam's, too.

"Spina de Mùl," Hannah corrected. She'd been watching the windows for the rotting mule sorcerer in his blue bath robe all

I GUESS SPINNING MULE GOT SOMEBODY!

morning. If she was Dolasílla, then that made the weirdo from the woods her arch-enemy. She was pretty sure kids her age weren't supposed to have arch-enemies.

The image of Rebekah and Asia conjuring new lies about her behind her back—Medusa hair and head lice and crushes on Adrian—flickered through her head. Her cheeks flushed even though the two girls were probably halfway to Disneyland by now.

Well, not destroyer-of-kingdoms arch-enemies, anyway.

The chainsaws shrieked again.

Mom pulled her hand away; her chair groaned across the floor as she stood up.

"I think it's time to get out of here. Come on. Up, up, up!"

She clapped her hands until both Cam and Hannah got up and dumped their dishes in the sink.

"It's a gorgeous day outside. I've got some photos to shoot downtown and we can swing by the toy store. Maybe we can even get a treat to celebrate your first day of summer break."

Hannah hesitated.

"But what about Spina de Mùl?"

Mom shrugged. "The storm is over and apparently we have a squirrel army—"

"Congress of Marmots," Hannah corrected.

"—Congress of Marmots protecting us. I think we're safe for now."

After a relay of water bottles, bags, and shoes, the three Troyers stepped out into the midday sun. A miniature squirrel did a back flip in Hannah's chest at the "thunk" of her mother locking the door behind them. She took a deep breath and followed her mom down to the sidewalk.

Diana and Clark's minivan was missing from their driveway, but on the other side, Jemma and Odessa, their babysitter's moms, attacked their normally picture-perfect front garden with sharp tools. Apparently, Big Ben wasn't the only victim of the storm.

"Where you guys headed off to?" Jemma asked, waving a pair of garden shears exactly like the ones Hannah kept in her bag to trim her not-so-secret-anymore bower.

"Just into town to take a short break. I've got an article due by tonight," Bridget replied.

"What's this one about?" Odessa asked.

"Just more for the Hillsboro history series. Railroads and steamboats, all that."

Bridget didn't stop walking as she answered. Hannah glanced over to Cam. What? Mom not stop for a half hour to chat with Jemma and Odessa? Either this was going to be the fastest break ever or...

Or Mom was nervous, too.

Hannah waved back to her neighbors.

For a few seconds they walked on in silence. Then Cam bolted.

Hannah took off after him, her nerves demanding some kind of action. She heard Mom shout behind them, then the sound of her shoes smacking the sidewalk to catch up.

Together they stopped at the place where the neighborhood met the woods. Down the hill where the footbridge crossed Hamby Creek, small trees had split and fallen across the path on both sides.

"Wow," Cam said.

"Yeah," Hannah agreed. "I guess we'll be doing some climbing."

One by one they picked their way through branches that now faced the wrong direction.

Hannah pulled a twig out of her black ringlets and trotted forward to where Cam stood at the forest crossroads, looking down the path into the deeper woods.

She stopped beside him.

She knew what was down there.

"Can we, Mom?" Cam asked.

Bridget untangled the backpack from the last of the branches and stumbled over to where they stood.

"Heck no."

Cam wasn't deterred. "Come on, Mom. I just want to see it."

Hannah offered a silent nod. Would there be some sign that it all really happened? Not just the incredible storm, but the other things.

The things that didn't seem quite so real in the daylight.

"It isn't that far in," Cam urged.

Hannah grabbed her mother's hand and pulled. Soon they were walking down the narrow dirt path toward The Congress of Marmots.

When they reached the semi-circle of trees, she and Cam broke away from their

mother and ran to it, searching for claw marks, fur, anything that would make their memories true. Hannah ran her hand over the scratchy bark. Just plain ol' tree.

Nothing to remember the story by, the story of the Fànes, the story of Dolasílla, the girl who tried to save the Fànes, but who was betrayed by her own greedy father. The story told by a pair of royal squirrels—their black eyes deep with sadness—about the ancient girl Hannah was supposed to be.

But I'm just a kid!

So was Dolasílla.

Hannah moved to the stump and crouched down.

There it was.

A SMALL PUFF OF WHITE FUR.

With her small fingers, she reached between the sections of bark and pulled free a small puff of pure white fur. She stared at it, her heartbeat disturbing the quiet.

"But I'm just a kid," she whispered.

Mom came up behind her as she stood up and took the little piece of fur from her. Like the night before, she pulled both Hannah and Cam close to her and gazed up the slender trunks of the trees.

"What in the great green avocado am I going to tell your father?" she murmured.

That, Hannah realized, was a very good question.

A very, very good question.

Tonya would like to thank:

The talented and lovely Maya Lilova, the artist whose work graces these pages!

Thanks go to her editors Damien Macalino, Trixy Buttcane, Shannon Page, and Raymond Macalino who make it possible for her to communicate coherently with the outside world.

And to the kind and welcoming community of Hillsboro, Oregon, for sharing the inspiring secrets of its past.

And, of course, she would like to thank her family, Raymond, Damien, & Heléna Macalino, who gave her the time and opportunity to scheme great schemes.

Thanks

Maya would like to thank:

My partner, family, and friends who have enabled me to be who I am;

My various pets who constantly remind me;

And the masterful Tonya Macalino who has given me the wonderful opportunity to take part in this great adventure!

Collect all 10 Books!

The Gates of AURONA

Book I
The Gates of AURONA
INTO THE HARE WOOD
TONYA MACALINO • MAYA LUCIA

Book II
The Gates of AURONA
THE ANGUANA'S TALE
TONYA MACALINO • MAYA LUCIA

Book III
The Gates of AURONA
SPINWATCH
TONYA MACALINO • MAYA LUCIA

#4
Spirits of the Silver Screen

#5
The Curse of the Children

#6
The Gates of Auròna

#7
The Battle at Five Oaks

#8
Heroes and Legends of Hillsboro

#9
The Kingdom of The Fànes

The Gates of AURONA
CREATURES OF THE DOLOMITES

Check **www.TonyaMacalino.com** for release dates.

Made in the USA
Middletown, DE
01 June 2019